NEMESIS

LILLIAN P. TSO

TABLE OF CONTENT

INTRODUCTION

Going through a cool night with a handsome guy like Stephen felt great yet it turned out to be the ugliest of all encounters she might have.

Replays... Nightmares.. Restless evenings.. Unsteady feelings, all turned into her organization for quite a while.

Indeed, even under the watchful eye of the most magnificent male medical caretaker she had at any point known, Simon Jeff, will her broken heart be retouched?

Will things at any point return to typical? Regardless of whether she could be remotely steady will the tempest inside her at any point be quieted?

#SYNOPSIS

One innocuous discussion.

One sheep in wolf clothing.

One evening of heart destroying torment.

At the point when the breezes of destiny blew, **NEMESIS** came knocking at everyone's doorstep.

Chapter 1

She chomped at her full kissable pink lips. Her hazel eyes were fixed on the jugs of wine organized on the racks. She read the marks and checked the level of the liquor content on the wine bottles. She could have done without liquor; the severe, unforgiving stinging taste spurned her. How or why many individuals got dependent on it, she was unable to interpret. She filtered the racks once more, focusing on the organic product wine bottles. She settled on one and connected with it. At five feet six inches, she wasn't unreasonably tall, however was a little better than expected.

"Goodbye," somebody said behind her.

"Evening... ``She looked back and saw a tall dull brown thin man, she set out toward the counter, a jug of wine in one hand.

"That is a decent choice."

What is he alluding to? The wine? Could it be said that he is following me?

She grimaced. She welcomed the woman behind the counter and paid for the wine.
"I have tasted that specific wine. It is paradise on ice-3D shapes."
Is it true or not that he is still conversing with me?
She looked back and discovered him smiling.
"The name is Stephen," he loosened up his right hand. She turned around to the woman and gathered the container of wine enclosed by a vivid
polythene sack. She strolled towards the exit. He ventured out in front of her and opened the glass entryway. She feigned exacerbation. She could see that he was attempting to definitely stand out.
"Much obliged to you," she murmured and left. He followed her.
"Anyway, what's the name?"
She ended and went to see him, "Look Mister... "
"It's Stephen."

"Whatever... I am not in that frame of mind of trading names with outsiders," she began to leave.
"Sorry Miss... " he rushed after her, "I have been watching you since you ventured into the wine shop."
"Continue to watch," she detected a spa and strolled in, regardless of the group. She would do anything or go anywhere to move away from him.
"Could I at any point be your escort for now?"
"I don't require one," she picked a flier at the front work area.
"You never can tell. The Galleria is a major spot."
She shrugged and extracted her direction from the shop. She detected that he was right behind her.
"Quit following me," she glared back at him.
"Can't resist Miss, I simply need to get to know you."
"Not intrigued."
"Allow me an opportunity."

She murmured, quit strolling and went to check him out. He streaked a bunch of white teeth; not that white, a shade of rich white to be precise.
He overshadowed her, a little more than five feet eight inches. The fitted dark tee-shirt on him gripped to his earthy colored skin. The blue engraving on it matched the shade of his pants. His shoes, a couple of dark chuckles with white stripes made him look charming in an innocent manner. She looked through his grinning earthy colored eyes. He appeared to be nice, in the event that looks were anything to go by. In any case, she wasn't in that frame of mind of being cordial with individuals she scarcely knew, particularly in broad daylight places.
"I needn't bother with an escort, gratitude for the deal," she went to leave.
"Stand by!" he held her by the elbow.
"Try not to contact me!" she yanked her hand free and looked at him.
"I'm grieved," he moaned and lifted his hands, "I come in harmony."

She did whatever it takes not to snicker. She was helped to remember the discussion among Arnold and the Dark Angel in a film she watched quite some time ago.

She made a sound as if to speak.

"I'm on out. This is the motivation behind why I am here," she raised the wrapped container of wine.

"Gracious, OK. Indeed, it is a cool night, an ideal time for a stroll near the ocean."

"Well... enticing, at the same time, I will pass."

"Come on. I haven't been to the ocean side in some time. I would cherish some great organization."

She shook her head. The Galleria wasn't that far from the Bar Beach and Kuramo Beach. She looked at her wrist-watch.

"I need to go."

"Some place significant?"

"Indeed," she met his consistent gaze.

"Where?"

"Nothing of you should be worrying about," she peered toward him.

"Is that why you can't accompany me to the ocean side?"
"Indeed and negative."
He raised an eyebrow.
"I need to go," she looked towards the lift and saw a line. She stepped towards the step way. He walked her fast strides with his long walks.
"You really want to quit following me."
"A stroll near the ocean is all I request."
"I can't," she moved down the steps.
"You can."
"I have a family supper to join in."
"That isn't significant."
She peered toward him once more, "It is. It is a month to month thing."
"Extraordinary, you can go one month from now."
"No."
"What number of family suppers have you missed for the current year?"
"None."
"You see."
"I see nothing."

"I know an extraordinary person whose barbecued chicken is excellent."
She laughed.
"The chicken with broiled Irish potato and velvety harsh vegetable serving of mixed greens is a pleasant combo."
Her stomach made senseless clamors. The discussion of food was making her hungry.
"You really want to evaluate this person."
They got themselves away from the structure among the overflowing group.
"I don't have any idea."
"We won't remain long. We will go for a short walk on the cool sand; purchase the chicken and beverages and leave."
"O-kay."
"Incredible!" he bounced. His fervor was infectious. She began to giggle.
"Where do I leave my vehicle?"
"There is a region outside the ocean side. We can pay those hooligans to watch it."
"Truly?"
"Indeed. They will safeguard the vehicle."
"OK."

"Will we?"
She gestured and followed him across the bustling street.

XXXXX

Gabriel Patrick checked out his appearance in the mirror. The lemon shaded kaftan he was putting on didn't cover his pot stomach. The brilliant weaving had sufficient detail to cause an interruption; perhaps nobody would see his distending stomach. It was about time he got back to the exercise center. He had been delaying a rebound for years, a decade to be exact. A man of his age required continuous activity, nothing sensational. He saw his better half the second she emerged from the restroom. She was wearing similar clothing. He saw that she had make-up on. What was going on with all the quarrel? It was simply supper. They were feasting inside with their kids and not outsiders.
"Ladies... " he murmured softly.

On the off chance that he had his direction, he would have placed on a tee-shirt and some shorts, yet his significant other wouldn't have it. She was tied in with being satisfactory consistently. Her steady reason was, 'Consider the possibility that we had unforeseen guests.'

"Are you prepared?" Angella looked at him.

He gestured and turned around.

"Did Susan call you?"

He grinned at the notice of his most memorable girl's name. She helped him to remember his late mother. Unimposing, dull delicate chocolate skin, exceptional full pink lips, hazel eyes, oval face with the idiosyncrasy of a holy messenger. Assuming his mom was alive, Susan would have been her number one grandkid.

"Hi... " she saw his lost, far away look.

What is on his mind now?

He squinted and gazed at his significant other. His grin expanded. His young ladies got their lovely looks from her and his young men got their attractive features from him.

He trusted they wouldn't acquire his pot stomach. A scowl wrinkled his dim foreheads.
"Gabriel."
"Well... "
She made an effort not to lash out, "Did she call you?"
"Who?"
She flickered and gazed back at him. She wanted to toss something at him. He saw the aggravation in her dim eyes.
What did I do now?
"Did Susan call you?"
He shook his head.
"Everybody is here. She isn't."
"Truly?"
"Indeed. She normally arrives before any other person."
"She will be here," his number one kid was presumably getting a couple of things. She had a propensity for carrying something to the month to month family supper.

xxxxx

The cool sea breeze cleared over them. She shook and folded her arms over her thrilling casing. The short-sleeve cream pullover she was putting on was essentially as light as a plume. She trusted she wouldn't come down with a bug. She turned her head and discovered him gazing at her.

"What?"

"You are shaking like a leaf. I figure we ought to head back."

"Splendid thought."

He helped her to her feet.

"I am so full. I question on the off chance that I will actually want to eat anything at my folks' place this evening."

He raised an eyebrow, "Would you say you are still going there?"

"Indeed," she looked at her wrist-watch. It was a few minutes past eight, "They stay on the Island."

"Goodness... "

They strolled towards the exit. She held her pencil obedient red shoes in a single hand

and her red Mark and Spencer pocket in the other hand. The sand felt smooth and cool underneath her feet. She was happy she consented to come to the ocean side.

"Trust we can rehash this."

"Sure."

"I need your telephone number, email address, facebook account, twitter handle and whatever else you have."

She began to giggle.

"I'm not kidding."

"I'm starting to think you will follow me on the web."

"Obviously I am."

She laughed and met his charming earthy colored eyes. He was truly charming. She turned away. Assuming they become old buddies, perhaps something great would emerge from their relationship.

"Come, I have a thought."

"A thought?"

"Come... " he headed towards a gathering of large shakes that remained between Kuramo ocean side and Bar oceanside.

Where is he going at this point? The ocean side is abandoned. Individuals seldom go there.
She followed him and he assisted her with moving to the opposite side. She saw inadequate gatherings near the ocean.
"Do individuals actually come here?"
He gestured, "Assuming you need isolation, this is the spot to be."
"I heard that those white pieces of clothing Prophets fabricate wooden shanties on the ocean side."
"Indeed, similar to that bamboo hovel covered with covers," he pointed at a wooden cabin a couple of feet away.
"Goodness!"
"We should investigate."
"No!"
"Come on, would you say you are frightened?"
She shook her head. She glanced around. It was getting more obscure. Her family should be asking why she wasn't anywhere near. She wished she had called.

XXXXXX

Angella snacked at her food, her watch-full eyes were set on everybody at the table. Her significant other appeared to be partaking in his feast. He had purged his plate and topped off it. Her most memorable child, Francis, was situated nearest to him. He had likewise required a subsequent making a difference. He was the specific duplicate of his dad, with the exception of the pot paunch. Her subsequent child, Daniel, was a combination of both herself and her significant other. He wasn't quite so tall as his dad; he was her level, five feet seven inches. Ashley, her subsequent little girl and last kid was her definite duplicate. She was the tallest in the family and the prettiest of her young ladies. She grinned, however it blurred when she saw her most memorable girl's unfilled seat. Where could Osayuki have been?

"Did Susan call anybody of you?"

Gabriel witnessed his third youngster's vacant seat. Where could she have been? It was not normal for her to be late. He trusted she was OK.

Francis was indifferent about his more youthful sister's nonattendance. The last time he saw her was at the workplace on Friday. She was a grown-up. She was mature enough to deal with herself.

Daniel asked why his mom had brought his more youthful sister's nonappearance up. He was partaking in his feast, yet, presently, he had lost his craving. She was thirty for the wellbeing of Pete, not two years of age. He got his glass of newly pressed squeezed orange and took a long beverage.

Ashley looked at her mom.

Susan, Susan, it is dependably Susan. Susan this, Susan that, would she say she is the one to focus on? Haba!

She was happy that her senior sister wasn't anywhere near. It would soak in the idea that she was somewhat flawed all things considered. She had had enough of her at the workplace. For what reason should the pattern go on in her folks' home? She murmured and dropped the fork and blade. She drove the half-destroyed plate of food.

"I accept I am addressing individuals that have ears," Angella snapped.

Francis made a sound as if to speak, "Mum, she isn't a child. She will appear assuming she needs to."

"Precisely," Daniel added, "She will most likely call you sometime in the evening or tomorrow and make sense of why she was unable to make it."

"She is coming," Gabriel said.

His kids checked out at him which caused a commotion. Trust their dad to come to Susan's guard.

"She has never missed a family supper," Gabriel ringed.

"This is most certainly her most memorable time," Ashley played with her fork.

He peered toward her. He got his Iphone on the table and dialed her number. It continued to ring. He moaned and dropped the telephone on the table. He turned upward and met his better half's scrutinizing look.

"She didn't pick the call," Gabriel shook his head.

Ashley laughed. It appeared that her desires were working out as expected.

Angella scowled. It was not normal for her little girl not to pick her calls. Where might she at any point be?

Chapter 2

He maneuvered her into the bamboo cabin. It was dull, peaceful and void. She squinted her eyes. There was no type of furniture in the little space.

She thought about what kind of strict gathering was held in the cabin.

"Might we at any point go at this point?"

He shook his head and pushed her. She fell on the sand with a crash. He grabbed her sack, flung it, got her shoes, tossed it and nailed her down with his weight. Dread grasped her.

What's going on with him? Gone was the cordial search in his earthy colored eyes. It had been supplanted by a dull vile gaze.

"This evening, you are mine," he made an evil guttural snicker. It creeped her out. She battled for opportunity underneath him, however his grasp on her was firm and steel-like. The prospect of what could befall her that evening made her break out in sweat, notwithstanding the dry virus air.

Goodness God... Please help me!

He tore her pullover separated with one hand and raised her short earthy colored skirt. Her trepidation duplicated. She whimpered and battled him.

"Stay composed!" he struck her in favor of her face. The stinging aggravation made hot tears spout out of her eyes and spilled all around her face.

"Please... I beseech you... let me go... " she cried.

"Hello... ssssh... don't cry," he cleaned her wet face with her torn shirt.

"Please... " she argued.

"Ssssh... simply sit back and relax, I will be delicate," he licked her face. She felt wiped out in the belly. No man had at any point gotten that near her. She had chosen quite some time ago to protect herself and give her virginity to her better half as a gift. No matter what the enticements she had confronted, she had never gone past kissing a person. The prospect of losing her virginity to a complete outsider made something snap inside her.

"Someone help me!" Her scream surprised him. He attempted to cover her mouth, however she messed with him.

"Oof!"

"Someone heeeeelp!"

He slapped her two times on the two sides of the face, stopping her shouts. He looked towards the entry. There was no solid. He lost.

Nobody heard her.

"Nobody will save you, you are mine," he maneuvered off her bra and stuffed it into her mouth. The obscene search in his eyes made her

heart to pound inconsistently against her chest. He dropped his head and gnawed at her chest, in a steady progression. Her cries were smothered by the material in her mouth. He held her hands over her head and detached her clothing. He kicked her thighs apart and crashed into her. He met an obstruction inside. He pushed in further and rode her like a pony. Horrendous torments went after her nerve cells and spread all around her body like out of control fire.

xxxxx

Ashley tasted at the glass of wine and sat with folded legs on the couch. She gazed at the TV yet gave no consideration to it. She saw her folks talking in murmurs at a corner. Could it be said that they were as yet stressed over her sister? She snickered gently. Their ideal girl wasn't excessively wonderful all things considered. For as long as she could recall, her folks, particularly her dad, had spotted Susan. She wasn't as dull, tall and large as they all were. She was unique. Why was she so unique? She had heard that her senior sister seemed to be her late fatherly granny. What does that have to do with anything? Might the similarity at

some point be the base of her dad's bias towards her?
Foolishness!
She depleted her glass and wanted to crush it on the white painted wall. It would create a situation. Her dad would reprimand her and her mom could never allow her to hear its finish.
Mrs. Prim and Proper.
She endlessly murmured once more. Supper was finished; she could head home.
Daniel looked at the gold plated wall clock. It was half beyond nine. It had been a decent supper. It was surprisingly better since Susan didn't appear by any means. She didn't actually try to call. In any event, their folks possessed more energy for them. Assuming she had been near, it would have been about her. He would have been powerful. He rested back on the seat and attempted to stand by listening to the CNN program on the TV.
Francis moved toward his folks. They quieted down.

"I need to leave now. You know how the traffic is at Lekki."
"OK child," Gabriel gazed toward him.
"Drive securely," Angella grinned at him.
He inclined towards her and pecked her on the two cheeks.
"I need to go as well," Daniel came up behind his senior sibling.
"However, you live on the Island. For what reason do you need to leave now?" she guided her look at him.
"I have what should be done before 12 PM mum," he pecked her on the two cheeks.
"I figure I will tap out as well," Ashley moved toward her folks.
"I can't really accept that they are abandoning us," Angella looked at her better half.
He crushed her shoulder tenderly.
"Dad, mum, goodnight," she waved at them and followed her siblings to the front entryway.
"Drive securely, holy messenger," Gabriel waved back.

They watched their youngsters leave.

"I will call Susan in the future. She makes them make sense."

Gabriel grinned and rested back on the seat. Any place his girl was, he was certain she had a valid justification for not appearing that evening.

"It would be ideal for her to have called in the event that she realized she wouldn't have the option to make it," she muttered and stood up.

He gazed toward her.

"Check out the pressure Mrs. Grace went through today to ensure that supper was great. Her way of behaving is unsatisfactory."

He shook his head and held his tongue.

Ladies!

xxxxx

She lifted herself and sat up. Her torn shirt held tight her slight sandy chest like a piece of cloth. Her skirt was messed and covered with her own blood. She started to cry. She checked out the dull hovel and looked for her shoes and pack with her freezing hands. She tracked them down and attempted to get up. Her knees clasped. She fell on her bum and lifted herself up once more and stood. She held her shoes and pocket with one hand and attempted to keep the torn shirt intact with the other hand. She stumbled out of the hovel and saw two figures a couple of feet away. She rested up against the bamboo support point and shouted out for help. They glanced toward her, examining whether to move toward her or leave.

"Pleeeaasssse... help me... "

They traded looks and strolled towards her.

"Who are you?" one of them held onto her up.

"What are you doing here?" the other gazed right in front of her.

She didn't exactly comprehend what they were talking about. She wanted them to assist her with getting to the closest clinic.

How can she impart what she believed them should do?
"Or is this a prostitute?"
They traded looks once more.
"Maga no pay?"
"Brothers, make us slash our own spotless mouth."
"Right," they shook hands and drove her back into the hovel.
She overreacted and shouted. They held her down and destroyed the remainder of her dress. The truth of her circumstance occurred to her.
"Please... no! Please... "
One of them held her hands while the other mounted her. She saw that he had a profound scar on the left half of his dim face. The other had a deformed right ear. The two of them looked like punks. She probably pulled a rabble.
Goodness God! Save me!
The man with the scar slammed into her like a cow on heat, with the force of projectiles flying out of an assault rifle. Sooner or later,

she dropped and awakened when the subsequent man dominated. His hands were all around her, similar to a fortune tracker. He turned her over and had her from behind. Blinding torment made her heave for breath. At the point when she was unable to take it any longer, she surrendered to the haziness that immersed her.

She recovered awareness. It was dull and freezing. She attempted to move yet extreme agonies went after her body. She expected to leave the ocean side. She would have rather not fallen into some unacceptable hands once more. She got kneeling down and utilized her hands to look for her garments, shoes and pack. She didn't track down anything. She began to cry. She was unable to leave the cottage Unclad. She thought about the dusty filthy covers that covered the cabin. She slithered to the entry and pulled at one of the covers energetically. One fell on the sand. The residue that radiated from it made her begin hacking. She folded it over her body and did her fair share up by holding the wooden casing immovably. Each move toward succession, she strolled towards the exit. She came to the side of the road and halted the principal taxi that she saw.

"Lady, where are you going?"

She thought for some time. Would it be advisable for her to return home? Would it be advisable for her to go to the police headquarters? She really wanted clinical consideration. Their family specialist worked at Saint Nicholas clinic. It was adequately close. She trusted he was still working.

"Take me to Saint Nicholas."

"Clinic?"

"Indeed."

He opened the rearward sitting arrangement entryway. She opened the entryway and moved into the vehicle. She shut the entryway and lay back on the seats.

"Lady, are you alright?" he watched her through the mirror.

"Take me to the clinic, quick."

He eased the vehicle into the street and drove off. After ten minutes, he stopped at the emergency clinic entryway.

"Lady, here we are."

"Go in and request Doctor Bia."

"What type of problem is this? please pay me my cash and let me leave here."

She sat up, "If it's not too much trouble, go in and request Doctor Bia. He will pay you any sum you need."

He murmured and killed the motor. He got down, murmuring to himself, shut the entryway and rushed into the enormous compound. He got back with an older man in his fifties. The second the specialist saw her, he ran once more into the medical clinic and got back with two medical caretakers conveying a wheel seat.

xxxxx

The ringing of his telephone awakened him. He heard his better half murmuring. It probably woke her as well. He sat up and turned on the bedside light. He connected to the telephone which was on the bedside cabinet and picked the call.

"Hi... "

"I sincerely apologize for upsetting you Mr. Patrick."

"Specialist Bia... morning," he perceived the family specialist's voice.

"Morning sir, sir, Susan is here with us."

His heartbeat sped up.

"Sir, she is in a basic condition."

"What has been going on with my girl?"

"Sir, you really want to come immediately."

"I'm coming."

Etinosa sat up and saw the frenzy on her significant other's face, "What is it?"

He went to take a gander at her, "Susan is in the medical clinic."

"What?!"

"Call the driver; we want to arrive immediately."

She gestured and looked for her blackberry telephone which was under her cushion.
"Call the kids as well. They need to meet us at the medical clinic."
She gestured in understanding. He shut his eyes and said a quiet supplication.

xxxxx

Ashley got her blackberry telephone. It appeared whoever was calling her was frantic to certainly stand out enough to be noticed. She actually looks at the guest's I.D. It was her mom. She looked at the wall clock. It was past two. What was critical to such an extent that I couldn't stand by work when the sun rose?
"Hi... "
"Sabby, you want to meet us at St. Nicholas medical clinic."
She sat up. What was happening? Is it safe to say that she was sick or more awful, did her dad fall and be wiped out?
"Sabby... "

She loved it at whatever point her mum called her 'Sabby'. It seemed like a charm, "Mum, what is happening?"
"Your sister has been conceded?"
"Susan?"
"Do you have some other sister?"
Was her sister wiped out? Was that why she didn't appear for the family supper?
"Your dad and I are headed to the clinic. Meet us there."
She moved down from the bed. It would require her around fifteen minutes to get to the clinic from her place in Lagos Island. She considered calling her siblings. Her mom would have called them. She searched for her vehicle key. Where did she drop it?

xxxxx

Daniel got up. He had recently gotten a call from his mom that his younger sister had been admitted into the clinic. He didn't see the reason why he ought to be hauled there too. Might it be said that he was a specialist?

He flung his closet open. What was he going to wear?
Susan, Susan, Susan. It was consistently Susan.
He hit his clench hand on the wooden entryway.
"Oof!" he held his hand in torment. He could detect it as of now; being an extremely drawn out day was going.

xxxxx

Francis joined his folks and younger sister in the sitting area. It worked out that he wasn't the only one in a nightgown. His dad had a major dark coat over his green nightgown. His mom had a red long coat over her blue nightgown. His sister had a blue jean coat over her pink nightwear. They generally seemed to be participants for a sleep party.
"Have you seen her?" he sat close to his mom. She shook her head accordingly. Her

eyes were red. She probably was crying. He looked

at his dad. He looked more terrible. He coordinated his look at his younger sister who was situated behind them, tinkering with her telephone.

Daniel walked around, in a red tee-shirt and some pants and matching blue boots. He had his telephones in one hand and the way into his vehicle in another. He welcomed his folks and kin and sat next to his sister.

Gabriel raised his head and saw the specialist moving toward them. He took a long full breath.

"Great morning everybody," specialist Bia tended to them.

"Great morning specialist," they chorused.

"Susan arrived in a taxi before sunrise, Unclad, wounded and... we found that she had been attacked."

Angella covered her mouth with her right hand, smothering a shout. Tears moved down her smooth dim face.

"Attacked... " Gabriel rehashed. It was difficult to accept that something that grim could happen to his girl.
"The degree of the wounds in her confidential part showed that she had been attacked by more than one individual."
"What?!" Daniel leaped to his feet.
Ashley felt goose pimples creeping all around her body. She folded her arms over herself and attempted to hinder the frightening contemplations that overflowed her psyche.
"She had the option to affirm the rape before she floated into obviousness."
"Where did the cab driver get her from?" Francis overflowed with outrage. He abhorred sissies who called themselves men, men who took
benefit of ladies to fulfill their terrible sexual invasions.
"He asserted that she stopped him along the side of the road, by Bar oceanside."
"Bar oceanside?" Francis and Daniel chorused.

Specialist Bia confronted Nosakhare, "I have told the police. The cabbie has taken them to the spot he saw her. They vowed to proceed their examinations from that point."

He maneuvered his better half into his arms. She began to shout without holding back. She felt as though she planned to kick the bucket. Ashley gazed at her and felt sorry for.

She was unable to envision what they were going through.

"On the off chance that you are prepared, you can all see her now."

He helped his better half to her feet. They followed the specialist

down the corridor. Their youngsters strolled behind them with temperamental advances.

The specialist drove them into a confidential room. They found Susan concealed with swathes.

Ashley sat at the bedside. She was unable to envision what her sister had to deal with. She wouldn't wish something like this on her most horrendously awful foe.

She despised assault stories. She felt furious, hurt and powerless at the same time. She trusted her sister's aggressors would be gotten and dealt with.

"Much thanks to you for everything," Gabriel warmly greeted the specialist. Specialist Bia gestured and left the room.

Angella sat at the opposite side of the bed, "Goodness God... take a gander at my child," she sobbed.

Gabriel collapsed his hands across his chest. He was unable to keep down the tears once more. He let it stream unreservedly. His chest fixed in misery.

"Those rats will pay. I swear on all that I hold dear, they will pay!" Francis fumed.

Daniel looked at his senior brother, his annoyance was irresistible.

Chapter 3

She woke up. She believed she was some place recognizable. Might it be said that she was home? She attempted to turn on her side, however the agonies that went after her made her moan.

"She is conscious," Ashley declared. Her folks and siblings accumulated around the bed.

"How are you sweetheart?" her dad's voice felt like a demulcent, relieving every one of her throbs.

"Daddy... " she croaked. Her throat felt exceptionally dry. She began to hack.

"I think she could definitely use a beverage," her mom gazed at her most youthful girl. Ashley grimaced. For what reason would she say she was checking her out? For what reason can't another person get the beverage?

"Sabby... " her dad motioned toward her.

"A beverage it is... " she got up and rushed out of the room.

"How can you feel?" Angella sat adjacent to her little girl. She went to see her mom. Her eyes were red and she had a miserable look all over.
"I'm... in torments," she began to hack once more.
"Where is Ashley?" Francis looked towards the entryway with bothering.
"You will be a good sweetheart," Gabriel sat alongside his significant other and connected for his girl's hand.
Daniel remained at the edge of the bed. He continued to check his sister out. She appeared to be more slender, slight and delicate. He saw Ashley with the side of his eye; she was conveying a glass of water. Her mom gathered it from her. Gabriel assisted Susan with sitting up, while his better half gave her a beverage.
Francis watched his folks. Trust them to spot their number one youngster and spoil her to a daze. He shook the considerations away. He was expected to appeal to God for

her speedy recuperation, not licking injuries from way back.

She depleted the glass and lay back on the bed, "My vehicle... I left my vehicle outside the ocean side."

Gabriel looked at his most memorable sister.

He met his dad's look and gestured, "I will proceed to get it tonight."

The contemplations of what occurred at the ocean side obfuscated her psyche. She shut her eyes and attempted to close out the recollections. The vile search in Stephen's eyes, the way the hooligans gobbled her up, the trepidation that consumed her psyche and the aggravation that assumed control over her body detonated to her. She started to shout.

"Susan... " Angella shook her by the shoulder. She didn't answer, her eyes appeared to be lost and far off, similar to she was elsewhere. She was terrified and went to her better half.

Susan kept on shouting, holding her head and attempting to no end to stop the path of her unbearable contemplations.
"Sweetheart... " Gabriel climbed the bed and attempted to hold her. She winced at his touch and sat up. She held her head with two hands and her piercing occupied the room.
"I figure we ought to call the specialist," Ashley joined her sibling at the edge of the bed. Her sister's unexpected response had frightened her.
Gabriel motioned to his most memorable child. Francis dialed Doctor Bia's number on his telephone and ran out of the room.
"Susan... " she drew nearer to her little girl. She perceived her mom's voice and flew into her arms.
"Mummy!" She held onto her like her life relied upon it.
"Indeed, sweetheart. I'm here. I'm staying put."
"Mummy... " she cried, "I see them... I see every one of them," she sobbed.

"Being a good darling is going. Mummy is here. I guarantee you, I will not permit them to hurt you at any point down the road."
"Guarantee?"
"Indeed, sweetheart, I guarantee."
His eyes stung with tears. He got up and stumbled out of the room. Daniel watched his dad leave. He felt disheartened by his ruffling.
Ashley inspected her mom as she reassured her senior sister. Not a single one of them had eaten or gotten any rest since they got back from the emergency clinic that evening. How could they adapt to Susan's circumstance? She questioned if things could at any point get back to business as usual.

xxxxx

Specialist Bia calmed Susan and she nodded off very quickly. He pivoted and took a gander at them, from one to the next.
"All of you want to rest, eat and rest."

"How is she?" he was stressed over his little girl.
The specialist murmured and went to the dozing magnificence, "She will be fine. She will have a ton of episodes like the one you recently saw... bad dreams comprehensive."
"Ok!" Ashley overreacted.
"For how long?" Angella cleaned the tears all over with the rear of her hand.
He stood, "I can't say."
"What does that mean?" Francis collapsed his arms across his chest.
He coordinated his look at the young fellow, "I recommend you utilize an in-house nurture."
"What for?" Daniel looked at the specialist.
He gazed at the young man, and afterward confronted their dad, "The medical caretaker will steady her with a sedative at whatever point she has an episode or a bad dream."
"For how long?" Angella withered.
He went to take a gander at the old lady, "Until the episodes and bad dreams stop."

"Amazing!" Ashley rested up against the wall. Things were more regrettable than she suspected.
"Might you at any point assist us with getting an in-house nurture?" Gabriel confronted the specialist. He was prepared to do anything that it took to assist her with recuperating as quickly as could be expected.
"Indeed. She likewise needs to see a Psychiatrist once she is ready."
"Whatever for?" Angella got to her feet and confronted the specialist.
"Conversing with a Psychiatrist will assist her with off-stacking the burden upon her conscience and bring her some type of conclusion."
Angella started to shake her head. Her girl didn't require a psychologist. She wasn't insane.
"Mama, she wants to address somebody about what has been going on with her."
"We are her loved ones. She will address us," Daniel approached his mom and put a

hand around her shoulder. She tracked down solace in his signal.

The specialist looked at the top of the family, "She wants a nonpartisan individual."

Gabriel gestured in arrangement. The analyst appointed to his girl's case additionally needed to talk with her. He questioned assuming that she was prepared to share her experience. Her brain appeared to be cracked. He was unable to comprehend what amount of time it required for the human psyche to mend and recuperate from such a shocking experience.

"I will make courses of action for the in-house nurture. She will be here first thing tomorrow first thing," specialist Bia headed towards the entryway.

"I will see you to your vehicle," Francis saw the specialist out. He had a ton of inquiries to pose.

"I figure you should both return home. You can determine the status of your sister

tomorrow," Angella congratulated her sister and looked at her
little girl. Daniel kissed his mom on the two cheeks and embraced his dad. He expected to rest. He probably won't go to work the following day. He was the top of the Accounts division in his dad's organization. He could call his right hand and cozy him on the best way to direct things in his nonattendance. Ashley followed her sibling out of the room. They met their oldest sibling at the vehicle stop. He was likewise on out.
Gabriel and his significant other left the room and shut the entryway tenderly. They trusted that Susan would remain quiet over the course of the evening.
"Is it true or not that you will work tomorrow?"
He put a hand around her shoulder, "As the CEO of Goldenberg Insurance Company, I must be there, no matter what."
She murmured vigorously.

"I will go frantic with stress in the event that I stay back at home."
"I will remain. I need to meet the medical caretaker and assist her with getting comfortable."
"Alright."
"I can't quit pondering... "
"About?"
"Where was God when our little girl was being attacked?"
He moaned and pulled her nearby in an embrace, "God is at any point present."
"In any case, "
"Ssssh... there are things we may in all likelihood never completely comprehend, in any case, that doesn't imply that God wasn't or alternately isn't there.
She breathed out uproariously.
"He never leaves or spurns us."
She realized he talked reality, yet, it was difficult to accept at that exact second.
"We will entrust the Lord with our entire existence and depend not on our own comprehension. In the entirety of our ways,

we will recognize Him and He will coordinate our ways," he summarized the third part of the book of Proverbs, stanza five and six.
She would attempt however much as could be expected to confide in God and rest in Him. All things considered, he sees the end all along. Her girl was securely in his arms, paying little mind to what she had gone through.

XXXXX

Specialist Bia sat in the parlor with his better half's younger sibling. They had been sitting tight for Mr. and Mrs. Patrick for over fifteen minutes. The House supervisor, Mrs. Grace, had let them know that the couple had recently awakened. He realized how depleted they were the other day. He anticipated that they should remain inside and rest.

Gabriel and Angella strolled into the parlor. They looked like a piece revived and noticeably drained.

"Great morning specialist," they chorused.

Specialist Bia and his brother-in-law got up and welcomed the couple. They got back to their seats, while the couple reclined across from them.

"I thought you said the medical caretaker will continue earlier today," she took a gander at the specialist then at the fair young fellow situated close to him.

He made a sound as if to say, "Indeed, em... this is Simon Jeff, my significant other's younger sibling. He concentrated on Nursing in London and he likewise has a certificate in Psychology."

Her dim foreheads wrinkled in a scowl. She got a brief look at her better half. His look portrayed dismay. They had both anticipated a female medical caretaker.

The specialist made a sound as if to speak once more, he could detect their dissatisfaction, "Simon is excellent at his

specific employment. He will offer both clinical and mental assistance to your little girl."
Gabriel and his better half evaluated the young fellow. They felt that a female medical caretaker would have been suitable.
"Might you at any point get us a female medical caretaker?" Angella guided her look at the specialist.
"I can vouch for Simon. Allow him to deal with your little girl for two or three days, on the off chance that you are not fulfilled, I will make a special effort to look for a female attendant."
Gabriel surveyed the young fellow. He looked as old as his most memorable child, "For what reason didn't you remain back in London?"
"I worked in various medical clinics back in London, be that as it may, I chose to return home to reward my country."
He grunted and got to his feet, "I'm off."
Specialist Bia and Simon rose.

"How about we find out what the young fellow can offer."
"Much obliged to you sir," the specialist said.
Simon saw that the moderately aged lady was gazing at him. He really wanted the job. Since he got back to the country quite a while back, his profits were nothing in comparison with what he acquired in London. His sister's better half had guaranteed him that the Paatrick family would pay liberally.
Mrs. Grace strolled energetically, "Sir, mama, she is alert."
They generally convoluted and checked her out.
"She is shouting her lungs out."
Angella overreacted. Gabriel scowled and looked at the specialist.
"Where is she?" Simon got his little pack and moved toward the lady.
"Accompany me," they rushed out of the room.

"She will be good. He will take great consideration of her," the specialist guaranteed them.
He loosened and pecked his better half on the cheek, "See you at night."
She moaned and watched them leave.

xxxxx

Ashley met her folks taking their supper when she showed up at the Patrick's ten room manor that night. She visited with them for some time prior to leaving for her sister's room. She met a fair young fellow taking care of her. She was shocked. Where could the attendant have been? The man was clad in a white casual shirt and pants. He seemed as though one of the male attendants in the sitcom 'Dim Anatomy'. He saw her presence and welcomed her. She gave a gesture and left the room. She rushed back to the feasting and sat down.

"I thought Doctor Bia should bring a female medical caretaker," she looked from one parent to the next.

"Male or female, as long as the person is a medical caretaker, I am fine with it," there was a note of conclusion in his voice.

"On the off chance that you say as much," she peered toward him and got a brief look at her mom. She looked fatigued.

"I didn't see you in the workplace today," Gabriel took a long beverage.

"I was unable to make the slightest effort when I got up today. I really wanted a three-day weekend."

Her siblings strolled into the room. They welcomed their folks and remained by the feasting.

"Have you both had your supper?" Angella looked through their countenances.

They gestured as one.

"Should Mrs. Grace carry you something to eat?"

"No, mum, much obliged," Francis sat down.

"I ate for certain companions on my way here. I'm full," Daniel grinned at her.
Mrs. Grace came in, welcomed her managers' kids and tidied up the table.
Simon went along with them and informed his new bosses that their little girl had been quieted for the evening and would before long nod off. They expressed gratitude toward him. He said goodnight and got back to his quarters, a room straightforwardly inverse of his patient's room.
"I believed Susan's medical caretaker should be a lady?" Daniel sat close to his sibling.
"Is it wise to utilize a male medical caretaker?" Francis checked the two guardians out.
"My point precisely," their sister added.
Gabriel guaranteed his kids that the male attendant was strongly suggested by their family specialist. They ought to all worry about their sister's speedy recuperation and not the individual dealing with her.

xxxxx

She lay on the bed in her nightgown. She had, had her supper and was trusting that rest will overwhelm her. It had been fourteen days since the occurrence at the ocean side. Her bad dreams came each and every evening. She trusted it would stop soon. Anything the male attendant quieted her with consistently quieted and tricked her back to rest. Her fantasies were generally fixated on the essences of the men that disregarded her. The torture worried her spirit and made it unthinkable for her to rest.

Master Jesus... will I at any point move past this terrible experience? Recuperate me Lord. Restore me once more.

Somebody thumped. She looked towards the entryway. The male medical caretaker opened the entryway, strolled in and made a couple of strides towards the bed.

"You are as yet conscious. I figured I ought to determine the status of you."

She moaned and turned on her side. He collapsed his hands across his chest. His senior sister's better half had educated him concerning her condition. He had dealt with individuals like her before. Many assault casualties lose their psyches because of their monstrous encounters. Some find it hard to relate with men.
Some became men critics. Others find comfort in lesbianism and an extraordinary number went to sex fiends. He asked that his patient would recuperate with every one of her resources flawless. The fact that she was a devotee makes it extraordinary. Her confidence in God would assist her with mending truly, genuinely and mentally. It would likewise help her through each challenge she could experience.
"Goodbye," he pivoted and found his way out.
She heard the entryway. She murmured once more and lay on her back. Efe had been exceptionally kind to her. On occasion, she heard him petitioning God for her. He was

dependably next to her at whatever point she had bad dreams. He would remain in her room until she floated off to rest. His presence was encouraging. She let out an uproarious yawn and turned on her belly. She flickered a few times and snoozed off.

Chapter 4

Gabriel sat in his enormous office. He had been running Goldenberg Insurance Company since he finished his childhood administration. He acquired the firm from his late mother. It used to be a little organization, in any case, throughout the long term, it had developed into a global foundation dealing with around the world. In a steady progression, his youngsters went along with him in running the organization quickly after they finished their administration year. He had set them accountable for various divisions, inside the circle of their ability. Susan had been remarkable. It didn't make any difference where he set her, she generally succeeded. Her knowledge and skill for business had urged him to place her responsible for everything. She resembled his second in order. His children had shown their dissatisfaction, in any case, he had no way out. Nobody could deal with the reins of the firm as she did.

It had been a month since she was gone after. She was by all accounts improving, at the same time, she was unable to continue work in her outlook. He had chosen to share her obligations among every one of his kids. He accepted with time, one of them could possibly fill in her situation until she acquired full recuperation and was prepared to get back to work. He trusted that when he resigned at eighty, she would assume control over the organization as the CEO. He heard a thump and looked towards the entryway. His significant other, children and most youthful girl strolled in. The ladies sat on the seats opposite the table while the men remained behind them.
"I feel that one of you ought to assume control over your sister's situation, until she gets back to work."

Daniel grinned from one ear to another. He had been trusting that his dad would go with that choice for a really long time. He accepted that he was fit for dealing with the situation as the second in order. His senior sibling gestured in concurrence with their dad. As the main child, he should be in charge, not his sister. Her circumstance had set out a freedom for him to show his dad that he was fit for running the organization. He saw that his younger sister was gesturing her head. Ashley was happy that her dad had found some peace with what had been going on with their sister. She accepted that she was equipped for taking over from her.
"In any case, the second in order position can't be messed with. There is a ton in question. This made me conclude that it is ideal assuming your sister's position is shared among you three."
His most memorable child glared. Francis could have done without offering titles and abilities to his kin. As the primary kid, it was his right. His younger sibling's grin blurred.

Daniel had believed that their dad would pick him. Their sister collapsed her arms across her chest. Ashley wouldn't fret offering powers to her siblings. Extra time, her dad would see that she was his most ideal choice.

"Much thanks to you for coming. You can all revisit your workplaces," Gabriel rested up against the calfskin seat.

His kids left the huge room in a steady progression. He met his significant other's satisfied look. He grinned back at her.

xxxxxx

Simon awakened around midnight. There was a weak sound behind the scenes. It seemed like somebody was crying.

Susan!

The possibility of her in trouble took him to leap up and run out of the room. He thumped on her entryway and opened it. He strolled in and saw her situated on the bed crying. The room was enlightened by the bedside light. He moved toward her and sat along the edge of the bed.

"Is it true that you are OK?"

"No!"

Her outrage didn't shock him. Her consistent bad dreams were sufficient to make anybody insane.

"Do I look OK to you?" she glared back at him.

He gulped hard, his eyes dashed sideways. On the off chance that attacking him would cheer her up, he was prepared to be her punching sack.

"Will I at any point be alright?" her tears-stained eyes zeroed in on his miserable ones.

He felt frustrated about her. He wanted to remove every one of her agonies.

"I continue seeing their faces... I continue to dream about what occurred... I feel like I am going off the deep end... in some cases, I think... self destruction may be the most ideal choice."

He shook his head, "No! No... " he moved nearer, "Never ponder doing that," his firm voice broke through to her.
"Yet, it is better than... "
"No!"
"I feel futile, spoiled, squandered, destroyed... " she put two hands on her head.
"Hello... don't say that."
"I'm worn out," tears started to stream once more.
He maneuvered her into his arms and shook her, preferring a child, "Ssssh... it is OK. Being good is going."
"Where was God when I wanted Him most?"
"He was in that general area with you."
"Watching?" her voice raised a pitch.
"Indeed, watching and ensuring that you didn't bite the dust at the time of your difficulty."
Her wet eyes lit up, "He saved me from death."
"Indeed he did."
"For what reason didn't he stop them?"

"There are a few things we may in all likelihood never completely grasp in this lifetime."
"Why?"
"I don't know Susan."
Her name all the rage soothingly affected her broiled nerves. She inclined toward him, breathing easy in light of the glow of his arms.
"I believe you should realize that God won't ever leave you or spurn you."
"Gee... "
"He feels your torments... "
"Ehn-hen... "
"He knows precisely the exact thing you are going through."
"O-kay... " she sounded sluggish.
Might it be said that she is dozing?
He hauled away and figured out that her eyes were shut. He put her on the bed delicately and attempted to get up. She mixed and opened her eyes.

"Try not to go... remain with me," the trepidation in her voice pulled at his heart.
"OK," he sat back on the bed.
She shut her eyes and curled into a ball. He murmured intensely. He would successfully make her terrible dreams vanish until the end of time. It had been two months since he had been dealing with her. Her family appeared to be happy with his administration. His probation period was certainly finished. At 35, he would have liked to work and earn substantial sums of money as a medical caretaker and a specialist. Sometime in the future, some way or another, he would set up his own facility and mental focus.
God it is all in your grasp now.
He peered down at her. It appeared she had nodded off once more. He got up and slipped away from the room.

XXXXX

Patrick's family sat at the feast, partaking in a tasty dinner of beat sweet potato and egusi soup with grouped hedge meat, smoked feline fish and barbecued pepper chicken. Quiet plummeted on the room when she strolled in, clad in a dark and red short night outfit with matching red low obeyed fighter shoes. She had on a medium length meshes twisted at the tips; the connection was a particular shade of brown. She welcomed her folks and kin, sat down at the feasting and started to dish her food. Her folks traded looks. It had been three months since the occurrence. They were satisfied that she looked well and had chosen to eat with them.

"How is the organization?" she guided her look to her kin, consistently, "I heard that my obligations have been separated among all of you," she tasted at her beverage. Francis looked at his dad then, at that point, back at his sister. On the off chance that they figured he would surrender his ongoing situation as the second in charge of the organization, despite the fact that he was imparting the title to his kin, they had something different coming. He was the main kid; he was where he should be in any case.

Daniel quit eating. He drove the plate away and got a brief look at his folks. They were energized that their number one kid was in a good place again. On the off chance that she figured she could get back to work and assume control over the reins of the organization, she better reconsider. He wasn't surrendering his current situation to anybody.

Ashley dropped her fork and blade on the plate and gazed at her senior sister, "You look well... "

"Much obliged to you," Susan grinned at her.

"Yet, do you think your brain is adequately normal to deal with the organization's business?" Ashley looked through her face. Her grin blurred. She gulped the food in her mouth and took a long beverage.

"Sabby, that is no real way to address your senior sister," her mom reprimanded her. Gabriel shook his head. On occasion, his youngest little girl regurgitated a ton of refuse.
"Let her be mum. She talks reality," Francis held his mom's stunned look.
"I agree," Daniel added.
Ashley grinned. The fact that her siblings upheld her makes her fulfilled.
Gabriel and his significant other traded looks. Were their kids ganging toward their sister? Is it true or not that they were disturbed that she was recuperating?
Susan drove her plate away. She could detect the intensity at the table. There were times she contemplated whether they maintained that she should be confined to bed until the end of the year. Sky preclude!
"Alrighty then, so what I heard is valid," she gazed at them.
Her younger sister looked at her. What had she heard? She looked at her siblings.

Daniel didn't mind any longer. He was prepared to battle for what was legitimately his.
Francis was burnt out on the preference in the family. He was prepared for war.
"I heard that all of you converted my situation in the organization, you have likewise held onto my vehicle and changed over my loft into a visitor house."
"Your vehicle and the condo are essential for the advantages of your work title... " Ashley ran through.
"Quiet down!" Her harsh tone cut off her younger sister's guard.
"Try not to advise her to quiet down. She is correct. You are in no state to run the organization. We have dominated," Daniel pummeled his clenched hand on the table.
"Valid, your things have been moved back to your dad's home. He can get you another vehicle and lease somewhere else for you," Francis added.
She pushed the seat in reverse and got up, "You have no right... not a solitary one of

you... no right by any stretch of the imagination," Susan gazed at them stonily.
"Enough!" Gabriel roared.
She saw her dad, "You permitted them to do this."
"It isn't that way," the hurt in her eyes disheartened.
She shook her head and walked out.
"Susan " her mom shouted toward her, however, she didn't answer. Angella went to check out her other youngsters. What had gotten into them all?
Daniel began to eat. He enjoyed the manner in which things had ended up.
Ashley grinned and murmured to herself. The most loved kid ought to return to her shell. She wasn't needed in their middle. Her residency was over.
Francis met his dad's irate gaze. He turned away and tasted at his beverage. That's what he trusted, assuming he permitted his dad to have his direction, he would make his

younger sister the CEO of the organization when he resigned. The time had come to prevent that from occurring.

XXXXXX

Susan found her dad's vehicle keys in his room. She took it and took off. She found her dad's dark Hummer jeep stopped in the typical spot, got in and crashed into the dull calm road. It was past eight. An hour drive would benefit her. She had one of her new telephones with her. She would have the option to arrive at Simon assuming need be. She ought to have called him before, yet, she had an inclination that he could persuade her not to take off from the house. Her vision became foggy. She cleaned her wet eyes with the rear of her hand. She resented each and every individual from her loved ones.

Minutes after the fact, she understood that she was out and about prompting Eko Hotel and Suites. She became frightened when she recollected that the ocean side was likewise nearby. She had been gone after on the oceanfront by somebody she scarcely knew and two hooligans. The obscurity of the night increased her domain of contemplations. Her heart dashed fiercely. She found a spot at the parking area outside Kuramo ocean side and left the vehicle. She got out and paid one of the young men staying nearby to watch it.

Her whimsical considerations pushed her towards Bar oceanside. She eliminated her red fighter shoes and moved over the gigantic rocks. The sand felt cool underneath her feet. Her heart roared against her chest. She started to feel a pestering migraine. She strolled around, searching for the bamboo cottage that was covered with covers.
What am I doing here? For what reason did I come here? I shouldn't have gone out.

She located the cottage a ways off and froze. She groveled and hurled. She took in lengthy in-take of breath and breathed out, it had a quieting impact on her nerves. She dialed Simon's number on her telephone and hung tight for it to ring.

"Hi... "

His voice facilitated her turbulent considerations, "Simon... come and get me."

"Susan, where could you be?"

"I'm at Bar oceanside."

"What on earth!"

"Come and get me."

"When did you take off from the house? I thought you were eating with your loved ones."

"Simon... "

"I'm coming. Attempt and unwind and inhale, alright, full breaths."

"Full breaths... " she rehashed and breathed in. She sat on the sand and trusted that he would come soon. She didn't know she would have the option to stroll back to the vehicle. She actually looked at the time on her telephone; it was nine o'clock straightaway.

xxxxxx

Simon found the Patrick family in the lounge area, contending.
"I'm sorry to upset you sir... " he moved toward Gabriel.
"It's OK," he motioned for him to come.
He bowed down and murmured into the sixty year elderly person's ear. His dull eyes extended in shock. He got up right away and got his telephone.
Simon made a stride back.
"Honey what is it?" Angella's stressed look caught his frightened face.
His eyes dashed at her, then, at that point, across the table. He pointed a denouncing finger at his youngsters.
"Your sister has jeopardized herself as a result of every one of you."

Ashley got to her feet. She looked at Simon, then back at her better half. She trusted Susan had not come to any damage.

"I will be right back," he gave his significant other a kiss on the cheek and rushed out of the room with the male medical caretaker.

She went to her kids, "Assuming that anything happens to your sister, I am considering every single one of you answerable," she looked at them and left the room.

Ashley murmured. She wanted to leave. She would prefer to be home perusing or watching Telemundo.

Francis sat back on his seat. He trusted his sister wasn't in any sort of peril. She had gone sufficiently through.

Francis folded his arms and gazed at his unfilled plate. He was all the while bubbling inside. He didn't mind at all what had been going on with his sister. He was worn out on his folks' steady consideration towards her.

xxxxxx

Gabriel and his little girl's medical caretaker showed up at the ocean side. He dialed her number and got a portrayal of where she was. After around ten minutes, they found her situated on the sand crying. Simon lifted her and cleared her up in his arms. He conveyed her back to his vehicle while her dad looked for his Hummer jeep. He tracked down it and paid off the young men that were watching it. Simon called Doctor Bia and hinted to him of her current condition. The specialist recommended that they ought to carry her to the medical clinic right away.

Susan heard individuals contending and battling their way off. She watched through the window and watched them. Simon saw the appearances all over. From the beginning, it was an inquisitive look, then acknowledgment, at the same time, it was supplanted by dread, torment then pain. He followed her look and saw two men battling. Unexpectedly, she began to shout. He leaped out of the front seat and joined her at the secondary lounge of the vehicle. She held her head with one hand and pointed at the men with the other. Her dad rushed to her side.

"What's going on?"

Simon pointed at the punks that were battling. He pursued his bearing. "I think she remembered them."

Gabriel gestured and dialed the quantity of the analyst responsible for his little girl's case.

Simon attempted to quiet her yet without much of any result. He wished he had brought along a sedative.

"Inhale... take long full breaths."

She gestured and shut her eyes. Her breathing came quick and hard. She had recently seen the men that went after her. Her psyche was going off the deep end.

Forty after five minutes, two formally dressed men showed up. Gabriel moved toward them and pointed at the criminals. They were all the while belligerence and

other rabble accumulated around them. The police officers isolated the men and hauled them towards Simon's vehicle.
"Do you know these men?" her dad pointed at the punks being held by the cops. She checked them out. One of them had a profound scar
across his face and the other had a deformed ear. She gestured rapidly.
"Daddy... They assaulted me. I asked them for help, at the same time, they assaulted me," she started to sob. He pulled her nearby and embraced her. He felt his blood overflowing with rage. Notwithstanding the presence of the police officers, he would have assumed control over regulations.
"It is OK sweetheart. They will pay for how they treated you," Gabriel motioned toward Efe and escaped the vehicle. The male medical attendant drew her nearby and helped her.

Gabriel called the investigator once more and insinuated to him what had occurred.

He gave one of the police officers his telephone and watched him speak with the analyst. The official returned the telephone and hauled one of the hooligans to their vehicle. His associate hauled the other along.

Simon and his supervisor set out for Saint Nicholas medical clinic.

Specialist Bia took care of her that evening and released her after he had affirmed that she was in a decent outlook.

Gabriel was amazed to meet his kids in the parlor when he returned home at around eleven. He thought they had returned home. They surrounded him, hungry for news.

Angella followed Simon to Susan's room and assisted him with settling her in for the evening.

"Simply express gratitude toward God for your sister's life. The two punks that assaulted her that evening have been gotten."

"Amazing! Acclaim the Lord!" Francis was feeling quite a bit better at the news.

"I will see the analyst tomorrow first thing. Those men will pay for the hopelessness they caused my girl," Gabriel said sincerely.
"I will accompany you father," Francis chipped in.
"OK, OK," he chose a seat. He was drained, yet feeling better at how the night had ended up.
"I will determine the status of her," Ashley left the room.
Daniel was as yet furious at how the family supper had finished. He contemplated whether Mrs. Grace had gone to sleep. He considered going to search for something to bite in the kitchen. He would need to go through the night in his folks' place. He was unable to return home, it was at that point late.
Angella sat alongside her girl. She had not let out the slightest peep since she was brought back that evening. Simon had described what occurred. She was appreciative to God that two out of the three men that attacked her had been gotten. She

chose to rest in her little girl's room that evening.
She believed that she should have a real sense of reassurance.
"It's OK," he motioned for him to come.
He bowed down and murmured into the sixty year elderly person's ear. His dull eyes extended in shock. He got up right away and got his telephone.
Simon made a stride back.
"Honey what is it?" Angella's stressed look caught his frightened face.
His eyes dashed at her, then, at that point, across the table. He pointed a denouncing finger at his youngsters.
"Your sister has jeopardized herself as a result of every one of you."
Angella got to her feet. She looked at Simon, then back at her better half. She trusted Osayuki had not come to any damage.
"I will be right back," he gave his significant other a kiss on the cheek and rushed out of the room with the male medical caretaker.

She went to her kids, "Assuming that anything happens to your sister, I am considering every single one of you answerable," she looked at them and left the room.
Ashley murmured. She wanted to leave. She would prefer to be home perusing or watching Telemundo.
Francis sat back on his seat. He trusted his sister wasn't in any sort of peril. She had gone sufficiently through.
Daniel folded his arms and gazed at his unfilled plate. He was all the while bubbling inside. He didn't mind at all what had been going on with his sister. He was worn out on his folks' steady consideration towards her.

xxxxxx

Gabriel and his little girl's medical caretaker showed up at the ocean side. He dialed her number and got a portrayal of where she was. After around ten minutes, they found her situated on the sand crying. Simon lifted her and cleared her up in his arms. He conveyed her back to his vehicle while her dad looked for his Hummer jeep. He tracked down it and paid off the young men that were watching it. Simon called Doctor Bia and hinted to him about her current condition. The specialist recommended that they ought to carry her to the medical clinic right away.

Susan heard individuals contending and battling their way off. She watched through the window and watched them. Simon saw the appearances all over. From the beginning, it was an inquisitive look, then acknowledgment, at the same time, it was supplanted by dread, torment then pain. He followed her look and saw two men battling. Unexpectedly, she began to shout. He leaped out of the front seat and joined her at the secondary lounge of the vehicle. She held her head with one hand and pointed at the men with the other. Her dad rushed to her side.

"What's going on?"

Simon pointed at the punks that were battling. He pursued his bearing. "I think she remembered them."

Gabriel gestured and dialed the quantity of the analyst responsible for his little girl's case.

Efe attempted to quiet her yet without much of any result. He wished he had brought along a sedative.

"Inhale... take long full breaths."

She gestured and shut her eyes. Her breathing came quick and hard. She had recently seen the men that went after her. Her psyche was going off the deep end.

Forty after five minutes, two formally dressed men showed up. Gabriel moved toward them and pointed at the criminals. They were all the while belligerence and other rabble accumulated around them. The police officers isolated the men and hauled them towards Simon's vehicle.

"Do you know these men?" her dad pointed at the punks being held by the cops. She

checked them out. One of them had a profound scar
across his face and the other had a deformed ear. She gestured rapidly.
"Daddy... They assaulted me. I asked them for help, at the same time, they assaulted me," she started to sob. He pulled her nearby and embraced her. He felt his blood overflowing with rage. Notwithstanding the presence of the police officers, he would have assumed control over regulations.
"It is OK sweetheart. They will pay for how they treated you," Gabriel motioned toward Simon and escaped the vehicle. The male medical attendant drew her nearby and helped her.
Gabriel called the investigator once more and insinuated to him what had occurred. He gave one of the police officers his telephone and watched him speak with the analyst. The official returned the telephone and hauled one of the hooligans to their vehicle. His associate hauled the other along.

Simon and his supervisor set out for Saint Nicholas medical clinic.
Specialist Bia took care of her that evening and released her after he had affirmed that she was in a decent outlook.
Gabriel was amazed to meet his kids in the parlor when he returned home at around eleven. He thought they had returned home. They surrounded him, hungry for news.
Angella followed Simon to Susan's room and assisted him with settling her in for the evening.
"Simply express gratitude toward God for your sister's life. The two punks that assaulted her that evening have been gotten."
"Amazing! Acclaim the Lord!" Francis was feeling quite a bit better at the news.
"I will see the analyst tomorrow first thing. Those men will pay for the hopelessness they caused my sister," Gabriel said sincerely.
"I will accompany you father," Francis chipped in.

"OK, OK," he chose a seat. He was drained, yet feeling better at how the night had ended up.
"I will determine the status of her," Ashley left the room.
Daniel was as yet furious at how the family supper had finished. He contemplated whether Mrs. Grace had gone to sleep. He considered going to search for something to bite in the kitchen. He would need to go through the night in his folks' place. He was unable to return home, it was at that point late.
Angella sat alongside her girl. She had not let out the slightest peep since she was brought back that evening. Simno had described what occurred. She was appreciative to God that two out of the three men that attacked her had been gotten. She chose to rest in her little girl's room that evening.
She believed that she should have a real sense of reassurance.

Chapter 5

She awakened and found her mom resting close to her. She yawned and loosened up her hands and legs. It had been quite a while since she had rested soundly. It seemed obvious to her that she had no bad dreams. She had rested soundly.
Much obliged to you Jesus.
She shut her eyes briefly and opened it. Assuming her evenings proceeded with that way, her full recuperation was showing sooner than she naturally suspected.
Somebody thumped. She looked towards the entryway. Simon opened it and strolled in.
"Morning."
"Morning," she sat up.
"Did you rest soundly?"
"Indeed, much obliged," she smiled.
"Would it be advisable for me to ask Mrs. Grace to bring you breakfast in bed?"
She shook her head, "I will clean up first. I figure I will eat at the feast."
"OK, great."

"Much thanks to you for coming to get me the previous evening."
"You are gladly received. In any case, the following time you need to take off from the house, out of the blue, simply call me."
"Alright. I will."
He ventured nearer, "I'm happy that you are OK. I was stressed over you."
She gestured, "I had no awful dream the previous evening."
He grinned, "I took note."
"I rested soundly."
"I'm happy," he could see the fervor in her eyes.
"God has addressed our requests."
"Indeed, he has."
They look locked. He was certain that surprisingly fast, she would have the option to return to her ordinary daily practice. He had seen that no man had come to investigate her. Is it true that she was single? He had found in her clinic records. She was thirty. For what reason would she say she wasn't in that frame of mind at that

age? Perhaps she permitted work to assume control over her public activity. He had seen that her kin were likewise single and work-driven. They generally expected to do a reevaluation. Life wasn't about work, cash and notoriety. There were different things that made it delightful and advantageous. Angella blended and woke up. She turned on her side and saw that her girl was conscious. She followed her look and saw Smon remaining by the entryway. For what reason would they say they were gazing at one another like that? She looked from one to the next. Have their relationship gone past medical caretaker and patient to a more private one? Was there something different happening between them? The young fellow was good and diligent. He would make a fine spouse for her compulsive worker girl who had not dated anybody since she moved on from the college. She made a sound as if to speak threefold.

Susan flickered and got some distance from the power of his look. She saw that her mom was conscious.
"Early daytime sweetheart."
"Mum, morning," she looked at her.
"Great morning mama."
She tossed a look at him and grinned, "Morning Simon."
For what reason would she say she was grinning at him like that? She was looking at him as though she had found something.
"Kindly, excuse me," he withdrew and left.
"Fine young fellow, right?"
She raised an eyebrow and her confused gaze caught her mom's energized ones.
"I think he is single."
She shrugged. She didn't have the foggiest idea what her mom was referring to.
"He will make a fine spouse for a fortunate lady."
Susan flickered, she didn't know why her mom offered such a remark.
The older lady began to chuckle. It was conceivable that the attendant and his

patient had no clue about what was happening between them. In the event that fate has smiled down from heaven, they would find out for themselves. She chose to avoid their business.

"What are you having for breakfast?"

"I don't have the foggiest idea. I will get a kick out of the chance to scrub down first."

"OK. I will tell Mrs. Grace to make you flapjacks and cereal."

"Sounds awesome," she got down from the bed and set out toward the restroom.

She lay back on the bed. It would be magnificent assuming her oldest little girl got hitched. Her fantasies about being a granny would at long last emerge. It could urge her different youngsters to settle down. Her most memorable child was 35. Her subsequent child was 33 and Ashley was 28. She was unable to recall the last time they presented anybody as they expected. They were centered around work, power and positions in her better half's organization. Did they commit an error in including the kids in the privately-run company? She switched off her line of considerations and did her fair share. She moved down from the bed and yawned. Her better half would have awakened. He probably saw her nonattendance from his side an evening or two ago. She grinned; he could manage without her sometimes.

XXXXX

Gabriel remained at the window, looking at the bustling road. He heard a thump on the entryway and turned around. Susan opened the entryway and ventured into her dad's office.
"Dear," he loosened up his hands.
"Daddy," she rushed into his arms.
He gave her a loving squeeze, "What are you doing here?"
"Visiting my daddy at work."
He delivered her, "Come... " he drove her to the sitting region opposite his work area, "How does it go with you?"

"I'm great. I'm here with Simon."
"Gracious! Truly?"
She gestured, "He is sitting tight for me in the vehicle. He is continuing work at Saint Nicholas clinic tomorrow."
"So I heard. He has been exceptionally useful."
She gestured in understanding.
"Is it true that you are additionally wanting to continue work?"
"Indeed, daddy."
"Great, great. I have a suggestion for you."
She raised an eyebrow. What was he doing?
"I believe that you should work for us as an expert."
Her foreheads wrinkled in a scowl.
"Listen to me," he lifted a hand.
She collapsed her arms across her chest and rested up against the seat.
"As an expert, you can work for as many firms as you can deal with. Your involvement with the business has instituted you as an extremely hot cake."
She laughed.

"A considerable lot of my companions have asked personal times without numbers to credit you to them."
"Goodness!"
"You have assisted us with developing and I accept that it is about time you cut a score for yourself in the business world."
She moaned. She had never pondered assembling her profession that way.
"Yet, you should bear in mind, Goldenberg Insurance Company starts things out."
"Don't worry about it."
"Much obliged to you for understanding."
"Much obliged to you daddy," she embraced him.
"Where are you and Simon off to?"
She delivered him, "Lunch."
"Lunch? At six PM."
She shrugged and got to her feet.
"O-kay. I surmise I will see you at home before 12 PM."
"The way that I am living under your rooftop for now doesn't imply that you can direct the way in which I go back and forth."

He put two hands on his belly and started to giggle.

"I'm not sixteen, dad, I am thirty."

He kept on chuckling.

"See you at home, at whatever point... " she walked out.

"Hello! These kids won't fix it."

Angella strolled in, "Honey, would you say you are prepared?"

"Ok... yes dear."

"I saw Susan."

"Indeed. She came by."

"Did you tell her?"

"Indeed, she acknowledged."

She came to sit close by, "Magnificent."

Somebody jumped into the workplace. They pivoted and saw Susan by the entryway, breathing quickly and hard. He jumped to his feet.

"Sweetheart, would you say you are alright?"

She looked back at him. Her eyes were wilted with dread, as though she had recently experienced her more awful bad dream.

Her mom hurried to her side. "What's going on here? What occurred?"

She held her mom by the hand and pointed at the opened entryway.

"Make some noise. What is it?" Gabriel's eagerness wasn't lost on her.

She gulped hard, "I saw him... " she murmured.

They traded looks.

"Who?!" Angella overreacted.

"He is in Daniel's office," she held her chest, trying in any case her dashing heart.

It occurred to them that she was discussing the individual who tricked her to the ocean side and assaulted her before the punks saw her.

"Are you certain?" her mom put a hand on her temple, really looking at her temperature.

She gestured, ventured forward and imploded in the seat.

"Remain with her," he told his significant other and ran out.

A couple of feet from his child's office, he heard clearly voices. He animated his means and opened the entryway somewhat. He saw Daniel and a taller man holding each other by the collar. He snooped.

"I have proactively paid you."

"I really want to go out of the country."

"Do I seem to be a bank?"

"You will give me each penny I need, regardless of whether you like it."

"I have proactively paid you for the gig. You wrecked things. Did I request a discount?"

"How could I know that those gangsters will see her and do anything they desire with her?"

"It is all your shortcoming. Imagine a scenario in which they had killed her."

"Be that as it may, they didn't!"

"You want to leave and never return."

"Give me the cash I requested and I will vanish."

"You won't get a kobo from me."

"You lie!"

Gabriel ventured back. He was unable to accept the discussion he had caught wind of. He dialed the analyst number on his telephone and talked with him in a low tone. He hung up and opened the entryway. Daniel let go of the man when his dad strolled in.
"What is happening here?"
"Nothing father," he changed his collar.
"Is it true or not that you are certain? You were both going to choke each other a second prior."
"We will proceed with this later," the taller man attempted to leave, in any case, Gabriel hindered his direction.
"Nobody is going anywhere."
The man glanced back at Daniel.
"Father, let him go."
"Nobody is leaving until I know why you have chosen to transform my organization into a boxing ring," he shut the entryway and rested up against it.
"It is a confidential matter, dad."
"Sir, I need to go," the man argued.

"Nobody is going anywhere."
Daniel gulped hard and met the taller man's glare.
A few minutes after the fact, somebody thumped. Gabriel ventured away and opened the entryway. Two formally dressed men strolled in, trailed by a man in a dark suit, around six feet tall.
"Much thanks to you for coming as an investigator," Gabriel warmly greeted the six footer man.
Angella and Susan followed them in and remained by the entryway.
"Miss. Patrick, might you at any point bring up the one who assaulted you at the ocean side?" the investigator asked her.
She pointed at the young fellow standing two feet from her dad.
"Great, young fellow, you will now be taken to jail," the analyst confronted the young fellow.
Stephen escaped. The two cops pursued him and found him down the corridor and took him back to the workplace.

"Mr. Daniel, what is your relationship with this man?" the investigator asked him.
He broke out in cool perspiration, "He is a close buddy."
The investigator confronted Stephen, "Who is Mr. Patrick to you?"
"He was my course mate back in college. We reconnected at a companion's party last year and he requested that I assist him with getting his sister out of the way so he can turn into the second in command in his dad's organization."
Angella and Susan looked at Daniel. He bowed his head in disgrace.
"He paid me 1,000,000 naira."
"You are accompanying us to the station. You are an accessory to the wrongdoing carried out eight months prior at the ocean side by this man," the criminal investigator approached him and took him by the hand, "Assuming you become unfriendly, I will cuff you and drag you out of here like a creature."
"Father... " his voice shuddered with dread.

His dad dismissed and left.
"Father!" Daniel shouted out, stunned that his dad wouldn't act the hero.
Angella pulled her girl closer and drove her out.

Chapter 6

The Patrick family left the court hall. They looked as Daniel, Stephen and the two punks were driven into the police van and driven out of the premises. The gangsters and Stephen were condemned to a decade's detention, while Daniel got five years as an associate.

"This is your whole shortcoming," Francis went after his dad.

Gabriel went to check his most memorable child out.

"You are not a rejected mum," he frowned at her.

"This isn't the time or spot to... " Susan censured him.

"Quiet down!" he attacked her.

She gazed back at her senior sibling. What was off with him?

"This is similarly your shortcoming," he pointed a finger at her.

She shook her head.

"Since the day you were conceived, they dabbed on you like, similar to something that will break any moment."
She drew nearer to her folks. She could have done without the way that her sibling's explosion was drawing consideration.
"He is correct. It is your whole shortcoming, Madam most loved youngster," Ashley ringed in.
She dropped her jaw and gazed back at her younger sister. She traded looks with her folks. They were similarly shocked.
He confronted his folks, "Your consistent moderate long stretches of partiality towards her prompted Daniel's debilitated arrangement."
"We might have settled this as a family, however, no, you tossed your child into jail," Ashley added and scowled at them.
Simon mediated. He drove the older couple to their vehicle and taught the driver to bring them back home. Susan followed him into his vehicle and stalled crying. He drove out of the parking garage and turned the

vehicle into the street. After an hour, he left the vehicle and got out. He opened the side entryway and aided her out of the vehicle. She checked out and gazed back at him.
"What are we doing here?"
"Do you trust me?"
She gestured.
"Great, then, at that point, accompany me."
She took a full breath and breathed out noisily. She held his hand and permitted him to lead her into Bar oceanside. She wasn't happy. She didn't really comprehend the reason why he brought her there.
"This spot presented to you a great deal of torment and bad dreams. I need to fundamentally alter the manner in which you feel about coming to the ocean side by supplanting your terrible recollections with blissful ones."
She raised an eyebrow. What was he doing?
"I have dealt with you for around eight, nine months and we've been old buddies a while later."
"Indeed and I am thankful."

"I need more."
Her eyes locked on his firm, serious ones.
"I need to deal with you each and every day and until the end of time."
She flickered. What was he talking about?
"I need to use whatever remains of my existence with you. I need to become old with you close by."
Her eyes stung with tears. His words console and fulfill a longing profound inside her.
"I didn't have the foggiest idea when I began succumbing to you... it just occurred to me as of late that you have assumed control over my entire heart. I maintain that you should be mine and I need to be everlastingly yours," he connected with her shaking hands.
Tears moved down her face. Amidst the difficulties in her family, she could hardly imagine how something so lovely was going on to her.
"I love you, will you marry me?"
She grinned, "Indeed, indeed, I will."

He drew her into his arms. She held unto him, tracking down solace in the glow of his arms. She shut her eyes and opened them. She saw a
gathering of men a remote place off. They were chopping down the bamboo cabin and tearing it apart. She moaned with alleviation. God had addressed her requests in additional ways than she could count.

xxxxx

Daniel sat in his cell which he imparted to twenty others. His previous activities darkened his contemplations. He had permitted jealousy, desire and sharpness to assume control over his heart and lead him down a horrendous way. If by some stroke of good luck he could turn around the hands of time. How was he going to endure five years secured with all kinds of hoodlums? One of the Prison officials moved toward his cell and coaxed him. He got up and

approached the door. The fact that he had a makes him instructed
guest and was driven out of the cell. He followed the official to a corner. There were a few seats organized in the minimized space. He saw a portion of the detainees situated with their guests. A couple of Prison officials remained wary. He plunked down and paused. He saw his younger sister the second she strolled in with the male attendant. He wished the ground would open and swallow him. They moved toward him and sat on a vacant seat in reverse.
"You have only ten minutes," the official reported and ventured away.
She gazed at her sibling. He was in a green khaki shirt and shorts. His face was thick with facial hair and he looked pale. He had likewise lost a great deal of weight.
"What's going on with you?"
He raised his head and glanced back at her, "What are you doing here?"
She gulped hard and looked at Simon. He pressed her hand in a token of help.

"I... I need to... I believe you should know that... I have excused you."
He flickered a few times. Tears accumulated in his eyes and there was a sense of foreboding deep in his soul.
"You... you had your explanations behind... at the same time, I apologize."
He gestured and bowed his head. She has excused him. How on earth is that even possible? Was it conceivable? Did he merit it?
"Could I at any point come... to see you... once in a while?"
He gazed toward her and gestured. The tears came.
"Simon and I are getting hitched."
He grinned and gestured, he took a gander at the male medical attendant, "Deal with my sister."
"I will," Simon guaranteed him.
The official returned, "Your time is up."
Simon helped his life partner to her feet. They said farewell and left.

"You have another guest," the watchman informed him.
He cleaned his face with the rear of his hand. He was in cuffs. It made it troublesome. His folks showed up and he sucked in breath. They
chose the seat inverse of him.
"Take a gander at my child," she started to cry.
He stilled his feelings and turned away.
"Kindly excuse us, we didn't intend to cherish one of our kids more than the rest," his dad argued.
"We overdid it," she cried.
He turned his head and coordinated his look at them, "I'm sorry as well... I didn't intend to... I was simply attempting to stand out enough to be noticed... " he began to cry.
The official returned and pulled him up, "Your time is up."
"I pardon you," his voice broke.
"Much obliged to you," they chorused and got to their feet. They looked as the official drove him away. He looked back at them.

xxxxx

Ashley opened the front entryway. She collapsed her arms across her chest when she saw her folks at the entryway.
"To what do I owe this fantastic visit?"
They traded looks.
"Shout out."
It occurred to them that she won't permit them in.
"Sabby... we... we committed errors,"
Angella gazed back at her.
"Indeed, you did, for sure."
"We are grieved," they chorused.
"You are 28 years past the point of no return," Ashley ventured once again into her condo and attempted to close the entryway.
Gabriel stopped her, "If it's not too much trouble, excuse us."
She peered toward them. Their slip-up had cost her sibling five years detainment. It can't be scattered.

"We will compensate for everything. Regardless of the stuff, regardless of how long," Angella guaranteed her.
She murmured and permitted them in. They strolled into the lounge room and sat on a settee while she reclined across from them.
"You quit coming to work, you won't pick our calls... we haven't seen you in about two months."
"That is history mum. What is the way forward?"
The couple traded looks.
"We have gone to see your sibling?" Gabriel illuminated her.
"How is he?"
They moaned.
"I will converse with Francis. All things considered, you are as yet our folks."
"Much obliged to you," they got up, "Another person is here to see you."
Her bewildered look locked on their quiet ones, "Who?"
"Show restraint," they got themselves out.
Susan and Simon came in.

"Wow," she folded her legs, "Here comes the most loved kid and her medical attendant."
They clasped hands.
"Sabby... "
"Try not to call me that! You have no right."
She gulped hard, "I didn't request to be inclined toward my kin."
"Like genuinely?"
"I had no clue that it affected everybody."
"I thought you were shrewd."
"I'm heartbroken. I'm upset for denying you of the delight and honors connected to being the last kid in the family."
She rested back on the seat and peered toward her.
"Our folks ought to have spotted you... not me."
"It is OK. The harm has been done as of now," Ashley turned away.
"Could we at any point begin once again... as a family?" Susan inquired.
"Without Daniel?"
"He is incorporated."
"He is in jail."

"He is still important for us, albeit from far off."
"OK... I will address Francis and let him know."
"I will represent myself," he emerged from his concealing spot, "I agree with your arrangements. I figure we can all begin once again as a family."
She grinned and pressed her life partner by the hand.
"When is the wedding?" Francis confronted Simon.
"It is in December."
"That is a month and a half away."
"Ashley... "
"You can call me Sabby."
They generally began to snicker.
"Will you like to be my respectable servant?"
"Obviously."
"Fantastic!"
"Trust you don't have a best man," Francis tended to Simon.
"Not actually."

"Advise him to hold off for a while. I'm your best man."

They generally began to snicker.

Susanwas exceptionally glad that they had the option to figure out their issues and accommodate. God had without a doubt been devoted.

www.ingramcontent.com/pod-product-compliance
Lightning Source LLC
LaVergne TN
LVHW050315160826
845677LV00014B/3412

* 9 7 9 8 3 5 1 6 6 2 5 0 3 *